To my little weaver of words - Bess
D.C.

For Andrea
K.L.

First published in Great Britain in 2006 by Gullane Children's Books
This paperback edition published in 2006 by

Gullane Children's Books

an imprint of Pinwheel Limited
Winchester House, 259-269 Old Marylebone Road, London NW1 5XJ

3 5 7 9 10 8 6 4 2

Text © David Conway 2006 Illustrations © Karin Littlewood 2006

The right of David Conway and Karin Littlewood to be identified as the author and illustrator of this work
has been asserted by them in accordance with the Copyright, Designs and Patents Act, 1988.
A CIP record for this title is available from the British Library.

ISBN-13: 978-1-86233-641-4

Printed and bound in China

The Most Important Gift of All

David Conway • illustrated by Karin Littlewood

GULLANE
CHILDREN'S BOOKS

There was once a girl named Ama who lived in a village perched on the edge of a great valley in Africa. Ama's mama was having a baby and Ama was waiting in the village garden for some news.

"You have a baby brother," said Grandma Sisi with a warm smile when she came to the village garden, "and his name is Azizi, beloved one."

The rainbow of butterflies that had been fluttering about inside Ama's tummy now turned into feelings of excitement.

I have a baby brother, she thought.

That afternoon the people of the village came
with gifts to celebrate the birth of Azizi.

Ama also wanted to give a gift.
"*Give him love,*"
said Grandma Sisi, "that is the
most important gift of all."

That night Ama dreamed
of this important gift called
love
that she could give to her new
baby brother. She dreamed that
it was as soft as a white cloud so
that baby Azizi could sleep on it . . .

. . . then as bright as a shimmering star that
would always keep him from darkness.

The following morning, after Ama had fetched
water from the well, she set off into the great valley
to search for the important gift. Ama walked and walked.
Along the way she met a weaverbird perched on the branch
of an Acacia tree. Ama asked the weaverbird if it knew
where she could find the important gift called *love*.
But the weaverbird didn't know.

Ama carried on walking.
Along the way she met a
giraffe chewing leaves
from a thorn bush.
Ama asked the giraffe if
it knew where she could
find the important
gift called *love*.
But the giraffe didn't know.

Again, Ama carried on walking and searching, and along the way she met a wise old lion lazing in the warm afternoon sun. Ama asked the wise old lion if it knew where she could find the important gift called *love*.

"I can not tell you that," said the
wise old lion stretching his ancient
body, "but as sure as the smell
of rain carried on a dry wind,

you will always know

love

when you have found it."

Ama continued to search and search and search but night
began to fall and, not knowing her way back to the village, she
sat by the trunk of a Baobab tree and decided to wait till morning.
She was starting to miss her family, the warmth of her grandma's
smile, the caring hands of her papa and the comforting arms
of her mama that would gently lull her to sleep.

All that night Ama waited for the sun to wake from its dreams.

Then, from a shaft of morning light that coloured the landscape like a paintbrush, Ama noticed something – something walking towards her.

At first Ama could not tell what it was. But as it came closer and closer . . .

. . . it became clearer and clearer.
To Ama's surprise and absolute joy
she saw that it was her papa who
had set out in search for her!

Ama jumped up from under the
Baobab tree and ran into her papa's arms.
Ama's papa was so relieved to find her that
he wept tears of joy and picked Ama up and
carried her all the way back to the village.

Ama's family were so happy to have Ama
home again – that evening they celebrated
with a meal of chapatis and mandazis
that Grandma Sisi had made.

Then, when Ama's family had finished their
meal, they began to clap and sing songs.

Songs about the birth of new children
and songs about finding lost ones . . .

. . . and as the songs filled the hut and the
African night, and mingled with the stars . . .

. . . somewhere faraway in the
great valley a wise old lion stretched
his ancient body and sniffed the
dark night air, for there
was something in it, something
as sure as the discovery of
the gift of love . . .

. . . and then the rain came.

Other Gullane Children's Books for you to enjoy . . .

When Brian Was A Lion

Carrie Weston

Illustrated by
Francesca Chessa

The Show at Rickety Barn

Jemma Beeke

Illustrated by
Lynne Chapman

Ferdie and the Falling Leaves

Julia Rawlinson

Illustrated by
Tiphanie Beeke

Pugwug and Little

Susie Jenkin-Pearce

Illustrated by
Tina Macnaughton

The Star Who Fell out of the Sky

Ian Robson

Illustrated by
Ian Newsham